George-A-Greene, The Pinner of Wakefield: A Retelling

David Bruce

Published by David Bruce, 2022.

This is a work of fiction. Similarities to real people, places, or events are entirely coincidental.

GEORGE-A-GREENE, THE PINNER OF WAKEFIELD: A RETELLING

Table of Contents

Dedication

DEDICATED TO MY SISTER MARTHA

Martha wrote, "When I was working at Longaberger, I worked with a girl who had two children and was in the middle of a divorce. She was so worried about Christmas for her boys. I received a very nice Christmas bonus that year, and I went to my boss and started a donation fund for the girl. My boss told me later that she — my boss —delivered the money to the girl's mother and father and told them not to tell her who brought the money for her. Months later the girl told me that the boys had the best Christmas that year, and she told me someone had brought money to her mom and dad for her, and she went to town and bought the boys Christmas. She never did know who did that for her. She was so thankful. I believe that I was the only one who donated to her, which was just fine."

***

The doing of good deeds is important. As a free person, you can choose to live your life as a good person or as a bad person. To be a good person, do good deeds. To be a bad person, do bad deeds. If you do good deeds, you will become good. If you do bad deeds, you will become bad. To become the person you want to be, act as if you already are that kind of person. Each of us chooses what kind of person we will become. To become a good person, do the things a good person does. To become a bad person, do the things a bad person does. The opportunity to take action to become the kind of person you want to be is yours.

Front Cover Photo for *George-A-Greene, The Pinner of Wakefield*: A Retelling:
https://pixabay.com/photos/man-vendor-caucasian-smile-seller-962565/

***

Anonymous. *George-A-Greene,*
   The Pinner of Wakefield:
   Earliest Extant Edition: 1599

Educate Yourself
Read Like A Wolf Eats
Be Excellent to Each Other
Books Then, Books Now, Books Forever

***

Do you know a language other than English? If you do, I give you permission to translate this book, copyright your translation, publish or self-publish it, and keep all the royalties for yourself. (Do give me credit, of course, for the original retelling.)

I would like to see my retellings of classic literature used in schools, so I give permission to the country of Finland (and all other countries) to give copies of this book to all students forever. I also give permission to the state of Texas (and all other states) to give copies of this book to all students forever. I also give permission to all teachers to give copies of this book to all students forever.

Teachers need not actually teach my retellings. Teachers are welcome to give students copies of my eBooks as background material. For example, if they are teaching Homer's *Iliad* and *Odyssey*, teachers are welcome to give students copies of my *Virgil's* Aeneid: *A Retelling in Prose* and tell students, "Here's another ancient epic you may want to read in your spare time."

CAST OF CHARACTERS

Edward, King of England.

James, King of Scotland.

The English Rebels:

Earl of Kendal.

Lord Bonfield.

Sir Gilbert Armstrong.

Sir Nicholas Mannering.

Other English Characters:

Earl of Warwick.

George-a-Greene.

Jenkin, George-a-Greene's serving-man.

Wily, George-a-Greene's serving-boy.

William Musgrove.

Cuddy, son to Musgrove.

Grime.

Bettris, daughter to Grime.

Jane-a-Barley.

Ned-a-Barley, son to Jane.

Main Justice of Wakefield. His name is Woodroffe.

Other Scottish Characters:

Lord Humes.

John Taylor, messenger to King James.

Robin Hood's Gang:

Robin Hood.

Much, the Miller's Son.

Will Scarlet.

Maid Marian.

Townsmen, Shoemakers, Soldiers, Messengers, etc.

***

HISTORICAL NOTES:

In the play, George-a-Greene meets and befriends Robin Hood, and so the time of the play is perhaps during the reign of King Richard I: Richard the Lionheart. (While King Richard I was away on a Crusade, Prince John, who later became King John, ruled England.) The anonymous author, however, uses the generic names Edward for the King of England and James for the King of Scotland. The anonymous author of the play does not much — or at all — concern himself with historical accuracy.

KING RICHARD I: 1189-1199

He was also known as Richard the Lionheart because of his military prowess as a leader and soldier. He was a Christian commander in the Third Crusade. As king, he spent little time in England. Much of his time was spent defending his lands in France. He also spent time in captivity.

KING JOHN: 1199-1216

He was also known as John Lackland because he lost the Duchy of Normandy and most of his lands in France. In 1215, he signed the Magna Carta. John is a bad man in Robin Hood stories.

OTHER NOTES:

A Pinner, aka Pinder, catches stray animals such as sheep and horses and puts them in an enclosed area called a pin-fold.

In this society, a person of higher rank would use "thou," "thee," "thine," and "thy" when referring to a person of lower rank. (These terms were also used affectionately and between equals.) A person of lower rank would use "you" and "your" when referring to a person of higher rank.

"Sirrah" was a title used to address someone of a social rank inferior to the speaker. Friends, however, could use it to refer to each other.

Thomas à Kempis (or Thomas a Kempis) means Thomas of Kempen (or Thomas from Kempen). Kempen is the town where he lived. Thomas à Becket (or Thomas a Becket) means Thomas of the Beckets; his father was Gilbert Beket. (Spelling was not standardized in the Middle Ages.)

George-a-Greene is George à Greene (or George a Greene), aka George of the Greenes.

• Peter Lukacs has an excellent annotated edition of the play at ElizabethanDrama.org:

http://elizabethandrama.org/the-playwrights/anonymous-plays/george-a-greene-the-Pinner-of-wakefield/

CHAPTER 1

— 1.1 —

The Earl of Kendal met with Lord Bonfield, Sir Gilbert Armstrong, Sir Nicholas Mannering, and John Taylor (a messenger of King James of Scotland) at the town of Bradford, about 300 miles north of London. Bradford was also about twenty miles from the town of Wakefield. All of these men were planning a rebellion against the King of England, and the Earl of Kendal was their leader.

"Welcome to Bradford, martial, warlike gentlemen, Lord Bonfield and Sir Gilbert Armstrong both," the Earl of Kendal said. "And to all my troops, even to my lowest servant, courage and welcome! For the day is ours. Victory is assured. Our cause is good: It is for the land's benefit. So then let us fight and die for England's good."

"We will, my lord," all the others said.

He replied, "As I am Henry Momford, the Earl of Kendal, you honor me with this assent of yours. And here upon my sword I swear to relieve the poor or die myself. And know, my lords, that James, the King of Scots, wars hard upon the borders of this land."

King James of Scotland was already fighting against the English counties bordering Scotland.

The Earl of Kendal continued:

"Here is his post-messenger.

"Tell us, John Taylor, what is the news regarding King James?"

"War, my lord, I tell, and good news, I believe," John Taylor said. "For King Jamy vows to meet you the twenty-sixth of this month, God willing; by the Virgin Mary, he vows this, sir."

"My friends, you see what assistance we have to win our fight," the Earl of Kendal said.

He said to John Taylor, "Well, John, commend me to King James, and tell him that I will meet him the twenty-sixth of this month, and tell him all the rest; and so, farewell."

John Taylor exited.

The Earl of Kendal said, "Bonfield, why do thou stand like a man in the dumps? Why are you melancholic? Have courage! For, if I win, I'll make thee a duke. I — Henry Momford — will be King of England myself. I will make thee Duke of Lancaster, and I will make Gilbert Armstrong Lord of Doncaster."

Lord Bonfield replied, "Nothing, my lord, makes me dismayed at all, except that our soldiers find our food scanty. We must make havoc against the local country peasants because if we do that the rest of the peasants will tremble and be afraid, and they will humbly send provisions to your camp."

The rebels needed to take what they needed by force. By making an example of a few countrymen, they could convince the other countrymen to give the rebels what they needed.

"My Lord Bonfield gives good advice," Sir Gilbert Armstrong said. "The country peasants scorn us and remain loyal to the King of England, so what provisions are brought to us are sent from them by force. Ask Mannering whether that is the case."

"What do thou say, Mannering?" the Earl of Kendal asked.

Sir Nicholas Mannering answered, "When I showed the countrymen your high commission demanding provisions, they made this answer: They would send provisions for your horses only."

"Well, hurry to the town of Wakefield," the Earl of Kendal said, "and tell the town to send me all the provisions that I want, lest I, like martial Tamburlaine, lay waste their bordering countries, leaving alive no one who won't fulfill my commission. Those who don't give me what I want will die."

Tamburlaine was an emperor who made war and ruthlessly killed those who opposed him and ruthlessly killed innocent people.

"Leave it to me," Sir Nicholas Mannering said. "I'll make them lower their plumes — their hats — and bow to you, for whoever he is — the proudest knight, justice of the peace, or any other man who refuses to carry out your order — I'll quickly take him prisoner, in order to make the rest fear to resist your orders."

"Do so, Nick," the Earl of Kendal said. "Hurry to Wakefield immediately and let us hear from thee again tomorrow."

"Aren't you going to move your camp, my lord?" Sir Nicholas Mannering asked.

"No, I will stay at Bradford all this night and all the next," the Earl of Kendal said.

He then said, "Bonfield, let's go and listen for news of some bonny lasses here."

— 1.2 —

At Wakefield, the main Justice of Wakefield, the other justices of Wakefield, some townsmen, and George-a-Greene were meeting with Sir Nicholas Mannering, who had presented them with his commission. Sir Nicholas was demanding provisions, and now the people of Wakefield were deciding whether to give him those provisions.

The main Justice of Wakefield said, "Master Mannering, stand aside, while we confer about what is best for us to do."

Sir Nicholas Mannering stepped aside.

The main Justice of Wakefield said to the Wakefield citizens, "Townsmen of Wakefield, the Earl of Kendal here has sent for food and other provisions. If we aid him, we show ourselves to be no less than traitors to Edward our king; therefore, let me hear, townsmen, what is your opinion."

The first townsman said, "Even as you please, we are all content. We agree with you that to help the Earl of Kendal will make us traitors to our king."

The main Justice of Wakefield then said to Sir Nicholas Mannering, "So then, Master Mannering, we have decided —"

Sir Nicholas Mannering interrupted, "— have decided what?"

"By the Virgin Mary, sir, we have decided this," the main Justice of Wakefield said. "We will send the Earl of Kendal no food and no other provisions because he is a traitor to the king; and in aiding him we would show ourselves to be no less than traitors, too."

Sir Nicholas Mannering replied:

"Why, men of Wakefield, have you grown mad, so that present and immediate danger cannot sharpen your wits and cannot make you wisely take action to save yourselves and your town?

"The Earl of Kendal's army is thirty thousand men strong, and whatsoever town resists him, he lays it flat and level with the ground. You foolish men, you seek your own destruction.

"Therefore, send my lord such food and provisions as he wants, so he will spare your town, and come no nearer to Wakefield than he is."

The main Justice of Wakefield replied, "Master Mannering, you have your answer. You may be gone."

Sir Nicholas Mannering replied, "Well, Woodroffe, for so I guess is thy name, I'll make thee curse thy hostile refusal to supply provisions, and all who sit upon the bench this day shall rue the hour they have rejected my lord's commission."

"Do thy worst," the main Justice of Wakefield said. "We don't fear thee."

"Do you see these seals on the commission?" Sir Nicholas Mannering said. "Before you cause the town to act against its own interests, I will have all the things my lord wants, in spite of you."

George-a-Greene, the Pinner of Wakefield, said, "You proud, dapper Jack, take off your hat to show respect to the bench that represents the person of the king. Or, sirrah, I'll cut off thy head and lay it before thy feet."

"Why, who are thou?" Sir Nicholas Mannering asked.

"Why, I am George-a-Greene, true liege-man and loyal subject to my king, who scorns that men of such esteem as these should endure the boasts of any traitorous squire."

George was insulting him by speaking to him in this manner. George was a yeoman, a rank lower than a gentleman. A knight ranked much more highly than a yeoman.

George then said to his fellow countrymen, "You of the bench, and you, my fellow-friends, neighbors, we are all subjects to the king. We are English born, and therefore Edward's friends. We vowed loyalty to him even when we were in our mothers' womb. We vowed our minds to God and our hearts to our king. Our wealth, our homage, and our bodies are all King Edward's."

He then said to the rebel Sir Nicholas Mannering, "So then, sirrah, we have nothing left for traitors except our swords, which are sharpened so we can bathe them in your bloods, and die fighting against you, before we send you any food."

"Well spoken, George-a-Greene!" the main Justice of Wakefield said.

"Please let George-a-Greene speak for us," the first townsman said.

George-a-Greene said to the rebel Sir Nicholas Mannering, "Sirrah, you get no food here, not even if a hoof of beef would save your lives."

A hoof has little, if any, edible portion.

"Fellow, I stand amazed at thy presumption," Sir Nicholas Mannering replied. "Why, who are thou who dares deny my lord, knowing his mighty power and the stroke of his sword? Why, my friend, I come not solely on my own authority. For, see, I have a large commission."

"Let me see it, sirrah," George-a-Greene said.

He took the commission and asked, "Whose seals are these?"

Pointing to the seals in turn, Sir Nicholas Mannering answered, "This is the Earl of Kendal's seal-at-arms. This is Lord Charnel Bonfield's, and this is Sir Gilbert Armstrong's."

George-a-Greene said, "I tell thee, sirrah, even if good King Edward's son should seal a commission against the king his father, thus would I tear it up in despite of him who is being a traitor to my sovereign."

He tore up the commission.

"What! Have thou torn my lord's commission?" Sir Nicholas Mannering said. "Thou shall rue it, and so shall all Wakefield."

"What, are you in choler?" George-a-Greene said. "Are you angry? I will give you pills to cool your stomach. Do thou see these seals? Now, by the soul of my father, who was a respectable yeoman when he was alive, eat the seals, or eat my dagger's point, proud squire."

The seals were made of wax; eating the seals would hurt only Sir Nicholas Mannering's pride.

George's father was a yeoman: a land-owning farmer.

George was threatening to stab Sir Nicholas Mannering.

"But thou do but jest, I hope," Sir Nicholas Mannering said.

Knights regarded it as beneath their dignity to fight people who were lowly born.

"To be sure, that you shall see before we two part," George-a-Greene said.

"Well, if there is no remedy, I do so, George," Sir Nicholas Mannering said.

He swallowed one of the seals and said, "One is gone; please, no more now."

"Oh, sir, if one is good, then the others cannot hurt," George-a-Greene said.

Sir Nicholas Mannering swallowed the other two seals.

George-a-Greene said, "So, sir, now you may go tell the Earl of Kendal that although I have torn his large commission, yet out of courtesy I have sent all his seals back to him again by you."

"Well, sir, I will do your errand," Sir Nicholas Mannering said.

He exited.

George-a-Greene said to the main Justice of Wakefield and his fellow townsmen, "Now let him tell his lord that he has spoken with George-a-Greene, the right — true — Pinner of the merry town of Wakefield. I have medicine for a fool — I have pills for a traitor who wrongs his sovereign."

He then asked the main Justice of Wakefield and his fellow townsmen, "Are you content with this action that I have done?"

The main Justice of Wakefield answered:

"Aye, we are content, George, for thou have highly honored the town of Wakefield in cutting off proud Mannering so short.

"Come, George, thou shall be my welcome guest today, for well have thou deserved reward and favor."

— 1.3 —

In Westmoreland, William Musgrove and his son, Cuddy, talked together. Westmoreland is an English county approximately 60 miles south of Scotland and 100 miles northwest of Wakefield. William Musgrove and Cuddy were Englishmen, and they were loyal to King Edward.

Cuddy Musgrove said, "Now, gentle father, listen to thy son, and for my mother's love, who formerly was blithe and bonny in thine eye, grant to me one thing that I shall request."

"What is that, my Cuddy?" William Musgrove asked.

"Father, you know the ancient and recent enmity between the Musgroves and the wily Scots, who have taken an oath not to leave one alive who bestrides a lance."

The Scots had sworn an oath to kill even the children of the Musgroves — children who play by bestriding a stick and pretending it is a hobby-horse.

If "lance" is a code word for "penis," then the threat was that the Scots would kill every male.

Cuddy continued, "Oh, father, you are old, and waning, declining age is taking you to the grave. You are nearing death. Old William Musgrove, who once was thought to be the bravest horseman in all Westmoreland, is weak, and forced to rest his arm upon a cane, his arm that once could wield a lance.

"So then, gentle father, resign the hold to me. Turn over the family property to me. Give arms to youth, and honor to age."

William Musgrove said:

"Get lost, false-hearted boy!

"My joints do quake even with anguish of thy very words. Has William Musgrove seen a hundred years?"

He had reached 100 years old.

He continued:

"Have I been feared and dreaded by the Scots, so that, when they heard my name in any inroad into England, they fled away, and rode quickly back to Scotland? And shall I die with shame now in my old age?

"No, Cuddy, no. Thus I resolve: Here have I lived, and here will I — Musgrove — die."

— 1.4 —

At Bradford, where the rebel army was staying, Lord Bonfield, Sir Gilbert Armstrong, Grime, and Bettris (Grime's daughter) stood together. Grime had provided a good meal for the rebels Lord Bonfield and Sir Gilbert Armstrong.

"Now, gentle Grime, God-a-mercy — thank you — for our good meal," Lord Bonfield said.

"God-a-mercy" means "God have mercy." It was a way of saying, "Thank you."

Lord Bonfield continued, "Our fare was royal, and our welcome great, and since so kindly thou has welcomed, entertained, and fed us, if we return with fortunate victory, we will deal as friendly with thee in recompense for how you have dealt with us."

"Your welcome was just my duty, gentle lord," Grime said, "for why have we been given our wealth but to make our betters welcome when they come?"

Grime, who was loyal to King Edward of England, said to himself, "Oh, things are bad when traitors must be flattered! But life is sweet, and I cannot avoid flattering them. God, I hope, will revenge the quarrel against my king."

"What did you say, Grime?" Sir Gilbert Armstrong, one of the traitors, asked.

"I say, Sir Gilbert, looking on my daughter, I curse the hour that I ever begot the girl," Grime said, "for, sir, she could have many wealthy suitors, and yet she disdains them all, in order to have poor George-a-Greene as her husband."

As a Pinner, a catcher of stray animals, George-a-Greene was not wealthy.

Lord Bonfield, who was interested in Bettris, Grime's daughter, said:

"On that subject, good Grime, I have been talking with thy daughter, but she, in the quirks and quiddities — the idiosyncrasies — of love, sets me to school and tries to educate me because she is so over-wise and precocious."

He then said to Bettris:

"But, gentle girl, if thou will forsake the Pinner and be my love, I will advance thee high in society and will dignify your hair of amber — golden — hue. I'll grace your hair with a coronet made of pearl, set with choice rubies, small sparkling gems, and diamonds, planted upon a velvet hood, to hide that head in which two sapphires — your eyes — burn like sparkling fire.

"This will I do, fair Bettris, and far more, if thou will love the Lord of Doncaster."

The Earl of Kendal had promised to make Lord Bonfield the Lord of Doncaster if the rebellion were successful.

Bettris teased Lord Bonfield by saying:

"Ho-hum! My heart is in a higher place, perhaps on the Earl of Kendal, if that is him coming.

"See where he comes. He is either angry, or in love, for those must be the reasons why his color makes him look unhappy."

The Earl of Kendal and Sir Nicholas Mannering entered the room. Sir Nicholas Mannering had informed — with some exaggeration — the rebel leader about how he was treated at Wakefield.

"Come, Nick, follow me," the Earl of Kendal said.

"How are you now, my lord!" Lord Bonfield said. "What is the news?"

The Earl of Kendal replied:

"It is such news, Bonfield, as will make thee laugh, and fret thy fill, when you hear how Nick was treated.

"Why, the justices stand on their terms and will not change their minds and give us food and other provisions.

"Nick, as you know, is proud in his words. He laid down the law to the justices with threatening, boastful words, so that one justice looked at another, ready to stoop and bow down to us, except that a churl, one George-a-Greene, the Pinner of the town, came in and with his dagger drawn laid hands on Nick."

Sir Nicholas Mannering was exaggerating. The justices and townspeople had never been about to submit to and aid the rebels. And although George-a-Greene had made threats against Sir Nicholas, he had not drawn his knife or laid hands on him.

The Earl of Kendal continued:

"And by no beggars George-a-Greene swore that we were traitors."

George-a-Greene had made a serious oath. He had not sworn by beggars.

The Earl of Kendal continued:

"He tore our commission, and he made a threat, forcing Nick to choose whether to eat the seals or endure being stabbed.

"Poor Mannering, afraid, came riding here immediately."

Bettris said, "Oh, lovely George, make Lady Fortune be always thy friend! And as thy thoughts be high, so be thy mind in all accords, even to thy heart's desire!"

Lord Bonfield said, "What is pretty Bettris saying?"

Grime said, "My lord, she is praying for George-a-Greene. He is the man she wants, and she will have no one but him."

"No one but him!" Lord Bonfield said. "Why, look upon me, my girl. Thou know that last night I courted thee, and I swore at my return to wed thee. So then tell me, love, shall I possess all thy beauty?"

"I don't care for an earl, nor do I care for a knight, nor for a baron who is so bold," Bettris said. "I do care for George-a-Greene, the merry Pinner. He has imprisoned my heart. It is no longer free to love anyone but him."

Lord Bonfield said to the Earl of Kendal, "It is useless, my lord, for me to make many vain replies to her. Let us hurry to Wakefield and send her the Pinner's head."

"It shall be so," the Earl of Kendal said. "We shall do that."

He then said, "Grime, gramercy — many thanks. Shut up thy daughter, keep her enclosed, and bridle her affections. Let me not miss her when I return; make sure that I see her. Therefore, look after her as you look after thy life, good Grime."

"I assure you that I will, my lord," Grime replied.

The Earl of Kendal said, "And, Bettris, leave a lowly born Pinner and instead love an earl."

Grime and Bettris exited.

The Earl of Kendal then said to himself:

"Gladly would I see this Pinner George-a-Greene.

"It shall be thus: Nick Mannering shall lead on the army in my absence, and we three — Lord Bonfield, Sir Gilbert Armstrong, and I — will go to Wakefield in some disguise.

"But one way or another, I'll have George-a-Greene's head today."

CHAPTER 2

— 2.1 —

Before the Englishman Sir John-a-Barley's castle, King James of Scotland met with Lord Humes and the messenger John Taylor. Some soldiers were present. John Taylor had given the Earl of Kendal's message to King James.

King James of Scotland asked, "Why, Johnny, then the Earl of Kendal is blithe and merry, and he has brave, splendid men who troop along with him?"

"Aye, by the Virgin Mary, my liege, and he has good men who come along with him, and he vows to meet you at Scrasblesea, God willing," John Taylor said.

"If good Saint Andrew, the patron saint of Scotland, grants me, King Jamy, permission, I will be with him at the appointed day."

Ned, the son of Sir John-a-Barley and his wife, Jane, entered the scene. Ned was a nickname for Edward.

Seeing Ned, King James said, "But wait a moment!"

He then asked, "Whose pretty boy are thou?"

Ned answered, "Sir, I am the son of Sir John-a-Barley. I am the eldest son, and I am all the sons that my mother ever had. Edward is my name."

"And where are thou going, pretty Ned?" King James asked.

"To seek some birds, and kill them, if I can," Ned said. "Now my schoolmaster is also gone, I have liberty to bend my bow and go hunting. For when my schoolmaster comes, I don't stir away from my book."

King James of Scotland said, "Lord Humes, just look at the face of this child. By the handsomeness of him, I guess the beauty of his mother. No one but Leda could breed Helena."

Leda, a beautiful woman, became Queen of Sparta. After being seduced (or raped, according to the source) by Zeus, King of the gods, she gave birth to Helen, the most beautiful woman in the world, who became Helen of Troy.

King James continued, "Tell me, Ned, who is inside with thy mother?"

"There is nobody but herself and the household servants, sir," Ned said. "If you want to speak with her, knock at this gate."

King James ordered, "Johnny, knock at that gate."

John Taylor knocked at the gate.

Jane-a-Barley appeared upon the walls of the castle and saw King James' army.

She said, "Oh, I'm betrayed! What multitudes of soldiers are these?"

King James of Scotland said, "Fear not, fair Jane. Don't be afraid, for all these men are mine, and all are thy friends, if thou will be a friend to me."

The word "friend" can mean "lover": He wanted to sleep with her.

King James continued:

"I am thy lover: I am one who loves thee. I am James the King of Scots, who often have sued and wooed thee with many letters, depicting my outward passions with my pen, while my inward soul did bleed for woe.

"Little regard was given to my love suit, but perhaps thy husband's presence wrought your little regard.

"Therefore, sweet Jane, I fitted myself to the time, and, hearing that thy husband was away from home, took advantage of the opportunity and have come to ask earnestly for what I long have desired."

Ned knew what King James wanted from his mother. King James wanted Jane to commit adultery with him. That would make Ned's father a cuckold: a man with an unfaithful wife.

"Nay, wait a minute, you, sir!" Ned said. "You get no entrance here, you who seek to wrong Sir John-a-Barley so and offer such dishonor to my mother."

"Why, what dishonor, Ned?" King James asked, either pretending not to understand or believing that Jane ought to consider it an honor to sleep with a king.

"Although I am young," Ned said, "yet I have often heard my father say that there is no greater wrong than to be made a cuckold. If I were of age, or if my body were strong — if I were older and stronger — I would shoot to the heart any man, even if he were ten kings, who would attempt to give Sir John the horn."

Cuckolds were said to have invisible horns growing from their forehead.

Ned then said, "Mother, don't let him come in. I will go and stay at Jocky Miller's house."

He would do that so his mother would not have to open the gate to let him reenter the castle. Opening the gate would allow King James to enter.

"Stop him," King James ordered.

His soldiers kept Ned from leaving.

"Aye, well said," Jane said to her son. "Ned, thou have given the king his answer. For even if the ghost of Caesar were on the earth, wrapped in the wonted glory of his honor, he would not make me wrong my husband so."

She then said, "But good King James is pleasant and is joking, as I guess, and he intends to test what mood I am in; otherwise, he would never have brought an army of men, to have them be witnesses of his Scottish lust."

King James began, "Jane, indeed, Jane —"

Jane interrupted, "— never reply, for I avow by the highest holy God, Who judges and gives just revenge for things amiss, that King James, of all men, shall not have my love."

King James said:

"Then listen to me:

"May Saint Andrew be my help, but I'll raze thy castle to the very ground, unless thou open the gate, and let me in."

The gate was both the gate of the castle and the "gate" that was her legs.

"I fear thee not, King Jamy," Jane said. "Do thy worst."

Normally, a king would be addressed as "you." Jane was disrespecting — justifiably — King James by calling him "thee."

Jane continued, "This castle is too strong for thee to scale. Besides, my husband, Sir John, will come home tomorrow."

King James replied, "Well, Jane, since thou disdain King James' love, I'll draw thee on with sharp and deep extremes. For, by my father's soul, I swear that this brat of thine shall perish here before thine eyes, unless thou open the gate, and let me in."

The "brat" was her son, Ned, whom he was threatening to murder.

"Oh, deep extremes!" Jane said. "My heart begins to break. My little Ned looks pale for fear."

She then said to her son, "Cheer thyself, my boy. Take heart. I will do much for thee."

"But not so much as to dishonor me," Ned said.

"But if thou die, I cannot live, sweet Ned," Jane replied.

"Then die with honor, mother, by dying chaste," Ned said.

Jane said, "I am armed. My husband's love, his honor, and his fame, enjoins victory by virtue. Virtue shall be victorious."

She then said, "Now, King James, if a mother's tears cannot allay thine anger, then butcher my son, for I will never yield: The son shall die before I wrong the father."

King James replied, "Why, then, he dies."

Battle trumpets sounded.

A messenger arrived and said to King James, "My lord, Musgrove is at hand."

William Musgrove was a long-standing enemy to King James and the Scots.

King James cried, "Who, Musgrove? The devil he is! Come, my horse!"

— 2.2 —

Later, before Sir John-a-Barley's castle, William Musgrove appeared with King James as his prisoner. Jane-a-Barley stood on the walls.

William Musgrove said, "Now, King James, thou are my prisoner."

"Not thine prisoner, but a prisoner of Lady Fortune," King James replied.

Cuddy, Musgrove's son, entered the scene and said, "Father, the battlefield is ours: We are victorious. We have seized their colors — their battle flags — and Lord Humes is slain. I slew him in hand-to-hand combat."

"God and Saint George!" William Musgrove exclaimed.

"Oh, father, I am very thirsty!" Cuddy said.

"Come in, young Cuddy, come and drink thy fill," Jane said. "Bring in King Jamy with you as a guest because all this broil occurred because he could not enter."

— 2.3 —

In the town of Wakefield, George-a-Greene, the town's Pinner, said to himself:

"The sweet content of men who live in love breeds fretting moods in a restless mind; and fancy, being checked by fortune's spite, grows too impatient in her sweet desires. Such desires are sweet to those men whom love leads on to bliss, but sour to me whose luck is still amiss."

Jenkin, George-a-Greene's serving-man, entered the scene.

"By the Virgin Mary, amen, sir," Jenkin said.

"Sir, what do you cry 'amen' at?" George asked.

"Why, didn't you talk about love?" Jenkin asked.

"How do you know that?" George asked.

Jenkin had overheard George's soliloquy.

"Well, although I say it who should not say it, few fellows in our parish are as nettled — stung — by love as I have been recently," Jenkin said.

"Sirrah, I thought no less, when the other morning you rose so early to go to your wenches," George said.

In this society, the word "wench" was not necessarily negative. It simply meant "young woman."

George continued, "Sir, I had thought you had gone about my honest business."

Jenkin had been chasing skirts instead of doing his job.

"Believe me, you have hit it when you talk about wenches," Jenkin said, "for, master, let me tell you, there is some good-will between Madge the souce-wife and I."

A souce-wife pickles edible parts of animals.

Jenkin continued, "By the Virgin Mary, she has another lover."

He had just said that there was good-will between Madge and him. A comic character, Jenkin frequently contradicted himself. He also sometimes made grammatical errors such as using "I" when he should have used "me."

"Can thou tolerate any rivals in thy love?" George asked.

Misunderstanding the word "rivals," perhaps deliberately, Jenkin said, "A rider! No, he is a sow-gelder and goes on foot."

A sow-gelder spays sows.

Jenkin said, "But Madge had an appointment to meet me in your wheat-close."

A wheat-close is a fenced — enclosed — area in which grain is grown. The fence kept out stray animals and some wildlife.

"Well, did she meet you there?" George asked.

"Never question that," Jenkin said. "And first I saluted her with a green gown, and afterward I fell as hard a-wooing as if the priest had been at our backs to have married us."

Appointments between a young man and a young woman often include an episode of the woman lying on her back and getting grass stains on the back of her gown.

"What, did she grant?" George asked.

Did she agree to marry him? Or did she agree to make out with him?

"Did she grant!" Jenkin said. "Don't doubt that. And she gave me a shirt-collar embroidered over with no counterfeit stuff."

"Was it gold?" George asked.

"Nay, it was better than gold," Jenkin said.

"What was it?" George asked.

"Right Coventry blue," Jenkin said.

Blue thread made in the city of Coventry was used in embroidery.

"We had no sooner come there but do you know who came by?" Jenkin asked.

Jenkin was contradicting himself again. Previously, he had said he had time to give Madge a green gown and to woo her.

"No," George answered. "Who?"

"Clim the sow-gelder," Jenkin answered.

"Did he come by?" George asked.

"He spied Madge and I sitting together," Jenkin said. "He leapt from his horse, laid his hand on his dagger, and began to swear."

Previously, Jenkin had said that his rival went on foot.

Jenkin said, "Now I seeing he had a dagger, and I having nothing but this twig in my hand, I gave him fair words and said nothing."

Another contradiction.

Jenkin continued:

"He comes to me, and he takes me by the bosom.

"'You whoreson slave,' said he, 'hold my horse, and make sure that he takes no cold in his feet.'

"'No, by the Virgin Mary, shall he, sir,' said I. 'I'll lay my cloak underneath him.'"

"I took my cloak, spread it all along, and set his horse on the midst of it."

"Thou clown, did thou set his horse upon thy cloak?" George said.

Cloaks were expensive.

"Aye," Jenkin said, "but note how I served him. Madge and he was no sooner gone down into the ditch, but I plucked out my knife, cut four holes in my cloak, and made his horse stand on the bare ground."

"It was well done," George said. "Now, sir, go and survey my fields. If you find any cattle in the corn, take them to the pound."

George's job was to impound stray animals. Here, he was delegating his job.

Jenkin said, "And if I find any stray cattle in the pound, I shall turn them out and release them."

Jenkin exited as the Earl of Kendal, Lord Bonfield, and Sir Gilbert Armstrong, all of them disguised, entered the scene with a party of men who served as their bodyguards. They did not see George.

"Now we have put the horses in the corn," the Earl of Kendal said. "Let us stand in some corner in order to hear what defiant terms the Pinner will breathe when he sees our horses in the corn."

They had set a trap for George. They planned to surprise him when he came to capture the stray horses.

The Earl of Kendal retired with the others.

Jenkin returned, blowing his horn.

"Oh, master, where are you?" Jenkin said. "We have a prize."

"A prize!" George said. "What is it?"

"Three excellent horses in our wheat-close," Jenkin said.

This society used the words "corn" and "wheat" interchangeably. Both words meant grain.

"Three horses in our wheat-close!" George said. "Whose horses are they?"

"By the Virgin Mary, that's a riddle to me," Jenkin said, "but they are there; they are velvet horses, and I never saw such horses before."

These horses were caparisoned in velvet cloth, and so their owners must be men of wealth and high social standing.

Jenkin continued:

"As my duty was, I put off my cap, and said as follows:

"'My masters, what are you doing in our close?'

"One of them, hearing me ask what he was doing there, held up his head and neighed, and after his manner laughed as heartily as if a mare had been tied to his girdle.

"'My masters,' said I, 'it is no laughing matter; for, if my master were to take you here, you would go as round as a top to the pound.'"

They would go round to the pound.

Jenkin continued:

"Another untoward — unruly — jade, hearing me threaten to take him to the pound and to tell you about them, cast up both his heels, and let such a monstrous great fart, that was as much as in his language to say, 'A fart for the pound, and a fart for George-a-Greene!'

"Now I, hearing this, put on my cap, blew my horn, called them all jades, and came to tell you."

Jades are bad horses.

"Now, sir, go and drive those three horses to the pound," George said.

"Listen to me," Jenkin said. "It would be best for me to take a constable with me."

"Why?" George asked.

"Why, they, being gentlemen's horses, may stand on their reputation, and will not obey me," Jenkin said.

For some wealthy people of high social standing, laws and rules are mild suggestions.

"Go, do as I tell you, sir," George said.

"Well, I may go," Jenkin said.

The Earl of Kendal, Lord Bonfield, and Sir Gilbert Armstrong now came forward.

The Earl of Kendal asked Jenkin, "Where are you going, sir?"

"Where?" Jenkin said. "I am going to put the horses in the pound."

"Sirrah, those three horses belong to us, and we put them in the wheat-close," the Earl of Kendal said. "And they must tarry there and eat their fill."

The Earl of Kendal lacked knowledge of horses. Eating too much high-starch grain can cause severe illnesses, including laminitus (founder), in horses. Horses can literally eat themselves sick — or dead.

Pinners help the owners of stray animals by keeping them from eating too much grain. Pinners also help the farmer who grow the grain.

"Wait, I will go tell my master," Jenkin said.

He said to George, "Do you hear, master? We have another prize: Those three horses are in your wheat-close still, and here are three geldings more."

Geldings are castrated horses, but as used by Jenkin, the word "geldings" referred to the Earl of Kendal, Lord Bonfield, and Sir Gilbert Armstrong.

"Who are these men?" George asked.

"These men are the masters of the horses," Jenkin answered.

George said to the three men, "Now, gentlemen (I don't know your social ranks, but you cannot be more than gentlemen, unless you are kings), why do you wrong us people of Wakefield with your horses? I am the Pinner, and, before you pass, you shall make good the trespass they have done."

Horses in a grainfield cause much damage and waste much grain. Food is valuable, and famines sometimes occur.

The Earl of Kendal replied, "Peace, saucy mate, don't prate to us. I tell thee, Pinner, we are gentlemen."

The word "gentleman" can refer either to a high social rank or to the possession of gentlemanly qualities.

The Earl of Kendal had said that the purpose of the rebellion had been to relieve the poor people, but his actions had not been evidence of that.

"Why, sir, so may I tell you I am a gentleman, sir, although I wear no arms," George said.

"Arms" can refer to a coat of arms or to weapons.

George had no coat of arms. He did own a staff.

"Thou!" the Earl of Kendal said. "How are thou a gentleman?"

The Earl of Kendal was behaving arrogantly, while George was showing gentlemanly behavior while insisting on his rights. George was calling the Earl of Kendal "sir."

Jenkin backed up George: "And such is my master, and he may give as good arms as ever your great-grandfather could give."

"Please, let me hear how," the Earl of Kendal said.

"By the Virgin Mary, my master may wear for his coat of arms the image of April in a green jacket, with a crow on one fist and a horn on the other, but my master wears his arms the wrong way, for he wears the horn on his fist; and your grandfather, because he would not lose his arms, wears the horn on his own head."

Horns on the head are the sign of the cuckold.

"Well, Pinner, since our horses are in the wheat-close, in spite of thee they now shall feed their fill, and eat until we are ready to go," the Earl of Kendal said.

"Now, by my father's soul," George said, "even if good King Edward's horses were in the corn, they shall pay for the damage, or kiss the pound."

As a loyal subject, George would not arrest the king, but he would impound the king's horses.

George continued speaking to the Earl of Kendal, "Much more yours, sir, whoever you are."

"Why, man, don't you know who we are?" the Earl of Kendal said. "We are the men of Henry Momford, Earl of Kendal, and we serve him. We are men who, before a month is fully expired, will be King Edward's betters in the land."

The Earl of Kendal was incognito. He was pretending to be one of his followers.

"King Edward's betters!" George said. "Rebel, thou lie!"

George hit him.

"Villain, what have thou done?" Lord Bonfield said. "Thou have struck an earl."

"Why, what do I care?" George said. "A poor man who is true and loyal to the king is better than an earl, if the earl is false and disloyal to the king. Traitors reap no better favors at my hands."

"Aye, so I think," the Earl of Kendal said, "but thou shall dearly pay for this blow."

He then ordered his bodyguards, "Now or never lay hold on the Pinner!"

They all came forward.

Seeing that he was badly outnumbered, George said, "Wait, my lords, let us parley on — talk about — these quarrels. 'Not Hercules against two,' the proverb is, nor I against so great a multitude."

He said to himself, "If your troops had not come marching as they did, I would have stopped your passage to London: But now I'll fly to secret policy."

George could not fight so many and succeed, but he could trick them.

"What are thou murmuring, George?" the Earl of Kendal asked.

"By the Virgin Mary, this, my lord," George said. "I wonder why, if thou are Henry Momford, Kendal's earl, that thou will do poor George-a-Greene this wrong: to match me against a troop of men."

George had guessed the Earl of Kendal's identity. He had been helped in this by Lord Bonfield's saying a little earlier, "Villain, what have thou done? Thou have struck an earl."

"Why did thou strike me, then?" the Earl of Kendal asked.

George said:

"Why, my lord, measure me but by yourself. Judge what I do by what you would do if you were in my position. If you had a man who had served you long, and this man heard your foe abuse you behind your back, and would not draw his sword in your defense, you would cashier — fire — him.

"Much more, King Edward is my king. And before I'll hear him so wronged, I'll die defending him within this place and back up as good everything I have said.

"And, even if you think that I am not speaking reasonably in this case, what I have said I'll maintain in this place."

"Give a pardon, my lord, to this Pinner," Lord Bonfield said. "For, trust me, he speaks like a man of worth."

"Well, George, if thou will leave Wakefield and travel with me, I'll freely put aside all you have done to me and I'll pardon thee," the Earl of Kendal said.

"Aye, I will, my lord, if you will do for me one thing: You will put aside these weapons and follow your good king."

"Why, George, I rise not against King Edward, but for the poor people who are oppressed by wrong," the Earl of Kendal said.

His actions had shown that this — helping poor, oppressed people — was merely an excuse for grabbing power.

The Earl of Kendal continued:

"And, if King Edward will redress the same, I will not offer him disparagement, but otherwise; and so let this suffice.

"Thou have heard the reason why I rise in arms: Now, if thou will leave Wakefield and travel with me, I'll make thee captain of a hardy band, and when I have my will, I will dub thee a knight."

"Why, my lord, do you have any hope to win?" George asked.

Warring against a king is a dangerous undertaking.

The Earl of Kendal replied, "Why, there is a prophecy that says that King James and I shall meet at London, and King Edward will take off his hat to us both."

"If this were true, my lord, this would be a mighty reason to rebel," George said.

"Why, it is a miraculous prophecy, and cannot fail," the Earl of Kendal said.

"Well, my lord, you have almost convinced me," George said.

He then said, "Jenkin, come here."

"Sir?" Jenkin said.

"Go on home, sir, and drive those three horses home to my house, and pour them down a bushel of good oats," George said.

"Well, I will," Jenkin said.

Jenkin, who was loyal to the king, then muttered as he left, "Must I give these scurvy horses oats?"

George said to the Earl of Kendal, "Will it please you to command your train of men to stand aside?"

"Stand aside," the Earl of Kendal ordered.

His men stood to the side.

George said:

"Now listen to me.

"Here in a wood, not far from here, there dwells an old man alone in a cave, who can foretell what fortunes shall befall you, for he is greatly skillful in magic art.

"You three go to him early in the morning and question him. If he foretells good things in your future, why, then, my lord, I am the foremost man who will march up with your camp to London."

"George, thou honor me in this," the Earl of Kendal said. "But where shall we find him out?"

"My serving-man shall conduct you to the place," George said. "But, my good lord, tell me truly what the wise man tells you."

"That will I, as I am Earl of Kendal."

"Why, then, to honor me, George-a-Greene, the more," George said, "deign to eat a piece of beef at my poor house. You shall have your fill of wafer-cakes, and you shall have a piece of beef hung up since Martlemas."

Martlemas was the traditional day for hanging up enough salted beef to last through the winter.

"Martlemas" is a now-obsolete word for "Martinmas," or St. Martin's Day, which is November 11.

George added, "If you don't like that, then I say that you can eat whatever you bring to my house."

"Gramercies, George," the Earl of Kendal said. "Many thanks."

They exited.

CHAPTER 3

— 3.1 —

Before Grime's house in Bradford, George-a-Greene's serving-boy Wily, who was disguised as a woman, and who had muffled his face to hide it, said to himself:

"Oh, what is love! It is some mighty power, else it never could conquer George-a-Greene."

He then said, "Here dwells a churl who keeps away his love."

Grime was keeping his daughter, Bettris, away from George.

Wily added:

"I know the worst, and if I am detected, the punishment is only a beating; and if I by this means can get fair Bettris out of her father's door, it is enough.

"Venus, especially for me, and all the gods above, aid me in my wily enterprise!"

Wily knocked at the door.

Grime opened the door and said, "What is this now! Who knocks there? What do you want? From where have you come? Where do you dwell?"

"I am, truly, a sempster's — seamstress' — maid, who lives nearby, who has brought work home to your daughter," Wily said.

He was saying that he had brought some work done by the seamstress for Bettris to examine and perhaps buy or order to be made in her size.

Grime was suspicious:

"Nay, aren't you some crafty quean — sneaky whore — who comes from George-a-Greene, that rascal, with some letters to my daughter?

"I will have you searched."

Wily replied:

"Alas, sir, it is Hebrew to me to tell me about George-a-Greene or any other! I do not know either Hebrew or George-a-Greene.

"Search me, good sir, and if you find a letter about me, let me have the punishment that's due."

"Why is your face muffled?" Grime said. "I like you less for that."

"I am not, sir, ashamed to show my face, yet I am loath that my cheeks should take the air," Wily said. "It's not that I'm particularly caring about my beauty's hue, but instead it's that I'm sorely troubled with a toothache."

Wily did not care if his face got tanned.

He unmuffled his face.

Grime looked at it and said to himself, "A pretty wench, of smiling countenance! Old men can like, although they cannot love, aye, and they can love, though not as brief as young men can."

A young man can finish love-making quickly; it often takes longer for old men to finish. Also, old men may need more time to seduce a woman.

Grime said, "Well, go in, my wench, and speak with my daughter."

Wily went into Grime's house.

Alone, Grime said to himself:

"I wonder much at the Earl of Kendal: Being a mighty man, as still he is, he is yet a traitor to his king. That is more than God or man will well allow. But what a fool am I to talk about him!

"My mind is more here on the pretty lass who just went into my house. Had she brought some forty pounds to town to be her dowry, I could be content to make her my wife. Yet I have heard it said in a proverb:

"He who is old and marries with a lass,

"Lies but at home and proves himself an ass."

Bettris, who was now wearing Wily's clothing and whose face was muffled, exited from the house.

Her father did not recognize her.

Grime said, "How are you now, my wench! How are things with you?"

Bettris remained silent, fearing that her father would recognize her voice.

"What! Not a word?" Grime said. "Alas, poor soul, the toothache plagues her sorely."

He then gave her a coin that was called an angel and said:

"Well, my wench, here is an angel for you to use to buy thee pins, and I ask thee to please visit my house. The oftener you visit, the more welcome you will be.

"Farewell."

He went inside his house.

Alone, Bettris said to herself:

"Oh, blessed love, and blessed fortune both!

"But, Bettris, don't stand here to talk of love, but instead hurry immediately to thy George-a-Greene. A roe-buck never went swifter on the downs than I will trip it until I see my George."

"Roe" is a species of deer. A buck is a stag: a male deer.

— 3.2 —

The Earl of Kendal, Lord Bonfield, Sir Gilbert Armstrong, and Jenkin talked together in a wood near Wakefield. They were going to visit the old man whom George had spoken of.

"Come away, Jenkin," the Earl of Kendal said.

"Come, here is his house," Jenkin said.

He then called to the old man, "Where are you? Ho!"

The old man, who was actually George-a-Greene in disguise, answered, "Who is knocking there?"

The Earl of Kendal said, "Here are two or three poor men, father, who would speak with you."

In this culture, people would often call an old man "father" even if the old man was not biologically their father.

The old man (George) replied, "Please, give your serving-man permission to lead me forth."

George, as part of his disguise, was pretending to be blind.

32

"Go, Jenkin, fetch him forth," the Earl of Kendal ordered.

Jenkin led forth the disguised George-a-Greene.

"Come, old man," Jenkin said.

"Father," the Earl of Kendal said, "here are three poor men come to question thee a word in secret that concerns their lives."

The Earl of Kendal, Lord Bonfield, and Sir Gilbert Armstrong were pretending to be men who were deciding whether or not to join the rebels.

"Say on, my son," the disguised George said.

The Earl of Kendal said:

"Father, I am sure you have heard the news about how the Earl of Kendal wars against the king.

"Now, father, we three are gentlemen by birth, but we are younger brethren who lack income."

This society followed the practice of primogeniture: The oldest son inherited the bulk of the estate. Younger sons received much less, if anything.

The Earl of Kendal continued:

"And for the hope we have to be preferred and raised in wealth and social rank that we know that we shall win if the rebellion succeeds, we will march with him, but if the rebellion will not succeed, we will not march one more foot to London.

"Therefore, good father, tell us what shall happen. Tell us whether the king or the Earl of Kendal shall win."

"The king will win, my son," the old man (George) said.

"Are thou sure of that?" the Earl of Kendal asked.

"Aye, I am as sure of that as I am sure that thou are Henry Momford, this man is Lord Bonfield, and the other man is Sir Gilbert Armstrong," the old man (George) said.

"Why, this is wondrous," the Earl of Kendal said. "Despite his being blind, his deep perceiverance — perception — is such as to know who we are."

"Magic is mighty and foretells great matters," Sir Gilbert Armstrong said.

He then said to the old man (George), "Indeed, father, here is the Earl of Kendal; he has come to see thee; therefore, good father, don't fable with him — tell him the truth."

"Welcome is the earl to my poor cell," the old man (George) said, "and so are you, my lords; but let me counsel you to leave these wars against your king, and instead live in quiet."

"Father, we haven't come for advice in war, but instead to know whether we shall win or lose," the Earl of Kendal replied.

"You shall lose, gentle lords, but not at the hands of good King Edward," the old man (George) said. "A baser man shall foil your plans and put an end to your rebellion."

"By the Virgin Mary, father, what man is that?" the Earl of Kendal asked.

"Poor George-a-Greene, the Pinner," the old man (George) answered.

"What shall he do?" the Earl of Kendal asked.

"Pull all your plumes, and sorely dishonor you," the old man (George) said.

Some helmets had plumes, and George would pluck them the way he could pluck the plumes — feathers — of a peacock. Doing that would humble the soldiers and the peacock.

"He will!" the Earl of Kendal said. "How?"

The old man (George) declined to give specific details as to how, but he emphasized that it would happen: "Nay, the end tries — proves — all; but so it will fall out."

"But so it shall not fall out so, by my honor Christ," the Earl of Kendal said. "I'll rouse my soldiers, and set on fire the town of Wakefield, and take that servile, menial Pinner George-a-Greene, and butcher him before King Edward's face."

"My good lord, don't be offended," the old man (George) said, "for I speak no more than my art of prophecy reveals to me. And for greater proof, give your serving-man permission to fetch me my staff."

"Jenkin, fetch him his walking-staff," the Earl of Kendal ordered.

Jenkin handed the old man (George) his staff and said, "Here is your walking-staff."

Casting aside his disguise and showing his true identity, George-a-Greene said:

"I'll prove that my prophecy is good upon your carcasses. You never yet met a wiser wizard, nor one who better could foredoom — foretell — your fall.

"Now that I have singled you here alone, I don't care although you are three to one."

The three rebels had come without their troop of bodyguards.

"Villain, have thou betrayed us?" the Earl of Kendal said.

"Momford, thou lie. I was never a traitor," George said.

He had not betrayed Henry Momford, the Earl of Kendal, because he had never joined the side of the rebels against King Edward.

George continued, "I devised this guile only to draw you on to be combatants. Now conquer me, and then march on to London, if you can. It shall go hard, but I will hold you to task."

In other words, stopping their rebellion might be hard, but nevertheless he would do it.

"Come, my lord, be cheerful. I'll kill him in hand-to-hand combat," Sir Gilbert Armstrong said to the Earl of Kendal.

"I will give a thousand pounds to him who strikes the stroke that kills!" the Earl of Kendal said.

He meant the blow that would kill George-a-Greene, but George said, "Then give the thousand pounds to me, for I will have the first stroke that kills."

The four men fought, three men against George, who killed Sir Gilbert Armstrong and made the other two men his prisoners.

"Stop, George, we do appeal," Lord Bonfield said.

"To whom?" George asked.

"Why, to the king," Lord Bonfield replied, "for we would rather endure what he appoints as our punishment rather than here be murdered by a servile, menial servant."

The punishment given to traitors was almost certain to be death. As a gentleman, Lord Bonfield was proud, and he preferred to be killed at the order of a king than to be killed by a commoner.

"What will thou do with us?" the Earl of Kendal asked.

"Just as Lord Bonfield wishes," George answered. "You shall go to the king. And, for that purpose, see where the main Justice of Wakefield is."

The main Justice of Wakefield had been hiding nearby to witness what would occur.

Coming out of hiding, the main Justice of Wakefield said, "Now, my Lord of Kendal, where are all your threats? Even as the cause, so is the combat fallen, else one could never have conquered three."

The reason for the rebellion was poor — the Earl of Kendal wanted to grab power, not to help the poor commoners — and therefore God had allowed George to fight against three gentlemen and be victorious. This had been a trial by combat, and God had helped the person who was in the right.

The Earl of Kendal said, "Please, Justice Woodroffe, do not twit and taunt me. If I have faulted, I must make amends."

"Master Woodroffe, here is not a place for many words," George said. "I beseech you, sir, to discharge all his soldiers, so that every man may go home to his own house."

Often, the soldiers of a rebel leader were pardoned and allowed to return home as long as they swore to be loyal to the king and to cause no more trouble.

"It shall be done," the main Justice of Wakefield said. "What will thou do, George?"

"Master Woodroffe, look after your responsibilities; leave me to myself," George replied.

"Come, my lords," the main Justice of Wakefield said.

Everyone except George exited.

— 3.3 —

Alone in the wood near Wakefield, George said to himself:

"Here sit thou, George, wearing a willow wreath, as one despairing of thy beauteous love."

Willow wreathes were a symbol of unrequited love. Bettris' father was keeping George from marrying Bettris.

He continued:

"Bah, George! No more. Don't pine away for that which cannot be. I cannot enjoy any earthly bliss, as long as I lack my Bettris."

Jenkin, George's serving-man, arrived and said, "Who sees a master of mine? Has anyone seen a master of mine?"

"What is it now, sirrah!" George said. "Whither away? Where are you going?"

"Whither away!" Jenkin said. "Why, who do you take me to be?"

"Why, you are Jenkin, my serving-man," George replied.

"I was so once indeed, but now the case is altered," Jenkin said.

He was claiming to no longer be George's servant.

"I ask thee, how is that true?" George said.

"Weren't you a fortune-teller today?" Jenkin asked.

"Well, what of that?" George asked.

"So surely I have become a juggler," Jenkin said. "What will you say if I juggle your sweetheart?"

A juggler is a magician; Jenkin was planning to conjure up Bettris for George.

Jugglers are also entertainers and tricksters.

"Be quiet, you prating losel! Shut up, you talkative good-for-nothing!" George said. "Her jealous father stands guard over her with such suspicious eyes that, if a man just dallies by her feet, he

37

immediately thinks that the man is a witch — a magician — who intends to charm and seduce his daughter."

"Well, what will you give me, if I bring her here?" Jenkin asked.

"An outfit of green clothing, and twenty crowns besides," George said.

"Well, give me your permission and give me room to work," Jenkin said. "You must also give me something that you have recently worn."

"Here is a shirt," George said. "Will that serve your needs?"

George gave him his shirt.

"Aye, this will serve me well," Jenkin said, drawing a circle in the dirt. "Keep out of my circle, lest you be torn in pieces by she-devils."

Normally, the conjurer will stay inside the circle. The dangerous devils are outside the protective circle.

Jenkin threw the shirt into the circle and conjured, "Mistress Bettris, once, twice, thrice!"

Bettris appeared from behind a tree where she had been hiding to surprise George.

Jenkin said, "Oh, isn't this cunning?"

It was not supernatural conjuring, but it did provide a welcome surprise for George.

"Is this my love, or is it but only her shadow?" George asked.

By "shadow," he meant apparition, aka ghost.

The day was sunny. Jenkin pointed to Bettris' shadow on the ground and said, "Aye, this is the shadow."

He then pointed to Bettris herself and said, "But here is the substance."

"Tell me, sweet love," George said to Bettris, "what good fortune brought thee here? For it was good fortune that favored George-a-Greene."

"Both love and fortune brought me to my George, in whose sweet sight is all my heart's content," Bettris said.

"Tell me, sweet love, how did thou come away from thy father's home?" George asked.

"A willing mind has many slips and tricks in love," Bettris said, "but it was not I, but Wily, thy sweet serving-boy, who came up with the trick."

Wily had acted without George's knowledge; he was a good servant.

"And where is Wily now?" George asked.

"He is still wearing my apparel, and he is still in my bed-chamber," Bettris said.

George ordered, "Jenkin, come here. Go to Bradford and listen for news about Wily, your fellow. What is happening with him?"

He then said, "Come, Bettris, let us go in, and in my cottage we will sit and talk."

CHAPTER 4

— 4.1 —

King Edward of England, King James of Scotland, Lord Warwick, Cuddy, and a train of attendants met in the court of King Edward in London. Kings called each other brothers even when they were not related either by birth or by marriage.

King Edward said to the captive King James:

"Brother of Scotland, I do take it hard, seeing that a league of truce was recently confirmed between you and me, that you should make such an invasion in my land without any displeasure offered to you first.

"The vows of kings should be as sacred oracles, not blemished with the stain of any breach, especially where fealty and homage will it."

Oracles foretell the future. A peace treaty should be like an oracle foretelling a period of peace between countries.

A person who swears fealty swears not to harm the person to whom he swears fealty. In the ceremony of homage, a person acknowledges that he holds his position at the pleasure of his overlord.

English kings continually wanted to be the overlords of Scottish kings.

King James replied, "Brother of England, don't rub the sore afresh: Don't remind me of what I have wrongly done. My conscience grieves me for my deep misdeed. I have had the worst; of the thirty thousand men in my army, there escaped not fully five thousand from the battlefield."

According to King James, he had lost twenty-five thousand soldiers in the battlefield. William Musgrove had led an English army against his.

King Edward said to Cuddy Musgrove, "Gramercy, Musgrove. Thank you, for otherwise the battle had gone hard against us. Cuddy, I'll reward thee well before we two part."

King James said, "But if his old father, William Musgrove, had not played twice the man — if he had not fought as well as two men — I would not now have been here in your court as a royal prisoner. A

40

stronger man I have seldom felt before; but a man of more resolute valiance — valor — does not tread, I think, upon the English ground."

"I know this well," King Edward said. "Old Musgrove shall not lose his hire. He will be rewarded for what he has done."

Luke 10:7 states that "the labourer is worthy of his hire" (King James Version).

Cuddy said, "And if it pleases your grace, my father was five-score and three at the last midsummer."

In other words, in the middle of the most recent summer, William Musgrove had turned 103 years old!

Cuddy continued, "Yet if King Jamy had been as good as George-a-Greene, my father, Billy Musgrove, still would have fought with him."

King Edward recognized George's name:

"As George-a-Greene!

"Please, Cuddy, let me question thee. Much have I heard, since I came into my crown, many people say as if they were reciting a proverb, 'Even if he were as good as George-a-Greene, I would strike him surely.'

"Please, tell me, Cuddy, if thou can inform me, who is that George-a-Greene?"

"Know, my lord, that I never saw the man," Cuddy said, "but mickle — much — is said about him in the country. They say that he is the Pinner of the town of Wakefield. But as for his other qualities, I will not speak of them."

Lord Warwick spoke up: "May it please your grace, I know the man too well."

"Too well!" King Edward said. "Why is that, Warwick?"

"Because he once beat me until my bones ached," Lord Warwick said.

"Why, does he dare strike an earl?" King Edward said.

"An earl, my lord!" Lord Warwick said. "Nay, he will strike a king, as long as the king is not King Edward. As for his stature and build, he is framed like the image of brave Hercules, and as for his carriage and bearing, he surpasses Robin Hood. The boldest earl or baron of your land who offers harm to the town of Wakefield by allowing his horse to eat its fill in a wheat-hold, George will arrest his pledge — his horse — and take it to the pound. And whosoever resists him carries away the effects of George's blows because George is as good a fighter by himself as are three men."

George would impound the horse and not release it until the damage the horse had caused was paid for.

King Edward said:

"Why, this is wondrous.

"My Lord of Warwick, badly do I long to see this George-a-Greene.

"But leaving him, what shall we do, my lord, in order to subdue the rebels in the north? They are now marching up to Doncaster."

A man arrived with the Earl of Kendal, who was a prisoner.

King Edward said, "Wait! Who do we have there?"

"Here is a traitor, the Earl of Kendal," Cuddy said, recognizing him.

"Aspiring traitor!" King Edward said to the Earl of Kendal. "How dare thou once cast thine eyes upon thy sovereign who honored thee with kindness, and with favor? But I will make thee pay dearly for this treason."

The Earl of Kendal began, "My good lord —"

King Edward interrupted, "Don't reply, traitor."

He then said, "Tell me, Cuddy, whose deed of honor won the victory against this rebel?"

"George-a-Greene, the Pinner of Wakefield," Cuddy answered.

King Edward replied, "George-a-Greene! Now shall I hear news certainly about who this Pinner is. Tell me briefly, Cuddy, how it befell."

Cuddy answered, "Kendal and Bonfield, with Sir Gilbert Armstrong, came in disguise to the town of Wakefield and there spoke ill about your grace. George, hearing their insults, felled them at his feet, and had rescue not come to the place, George would have slain them in his wheat-close."

Cuddy was exaggerating a little.

"But, Cuddy," King Edward said, "Can't thou tell how and where I might give and grant something that might please and highly gratify the Pinner's thoughts?"

He wished to reward George-a-Greene for his services to the crown.

Cuddy, who had earlier said that he had never met George-a-Greene, now said, "This at their parting George did say to me: 'If the king wishes to grant me something for my service, then, gentle Cuddy, kneel upon thy knee, and humbly crave a boon from him for me.'"

"Cuddy, what is it?" King Edward said.

"It is his will that your grace would pardon them, and let them live, although they have offended," Cuddy said.

King Edward said:

"I think the man strives to be glorious.

"Well, George has asked for it, and it shall be granted, which no one but he in England would have gotten."

He then said, "Live, Kendal, but as a prisoner. Thou shall end thy days within the Tower of London."

"Edward is gracious to offending subjects," the Earl of Kendal said.

"My Lord of Kendal, you're welcome to the court," King James of Scotland said.

They would be fellow prisoners until King James was ransomed.

King Edward said:

"Nay, not well-come, but ill-come as it falls out now."

The Earl of Kendal's coming to the court was ill for the Earl of Kendal because he was a prisoner.

He continued:

"Aye, it would be ill-come indeed, were it not for George-a-Greene."

If not for George-a-Greene, the Earl of Kendal would have arrived at the court seeking to depose King Edward. That coming would have been ill for King Edward whether or not Kendal's rebellion was successful. No king wants a rebellion.

King Edward then took off his hat and said ironically to King James and to the Earl of Kendal:

"But, gentle king, because you would like to claim that you are king over me, and because you would like to claim that you are Edward's betters, I salute you both."

Edward's "betters" were King James and the Earl of Kendal.

Earlier, the Earl of Kendal had said to George-a-Greene, "Why, there is a prophecy that says that King James and I shall meet at London, and King Edward will take off his hat to us both."

King Edward then put on his hat and said unironically:

"And here I vow by good Saint George, patron saint of England, that you will gain but little when your sums are counted."

They had lost more than they had gained by warring against King Edward.

He continued:

"I very much long to see this George-a-Greene, and because I have never seen the north of England, I will immediately go and see it, and so that no one will know who I am, we will disguise ourselves and steal down secretly, King James — thou and I, Cuddy, and two or three more — and we will make a merry journey for a month.

"Away, then, conduct the Earl of Kendal to the Tower of London.

"Come on, King James, my heart must necessarily be merry, if Fortune makes such havoc of our foes."

— 4.2 —

In Robin Hood's retreat, Robin Hood, Maid Marian, Will Scarlet, and Much the Miller's son talked together. The word "Maid" in "Maid Marian" meant "maiden" — a young woman.

"Why isn't lovely Marian blithe and cheerful? What ails my leman — my sweetheart — so that she begins to frown? Tell me, good Marian, why are thou so sad?"

"Nothing, my Robin, grieves me to the heart except that, whenever I walk abroad, I hear no songs at all except songs about George-a-Greene,"

Maid Marian said. "Bettris, his fair sweetheart, surpasses me, and this, my Robin, galls and irritates my very soul."

"Be content and happy," Robin said. "What does it matter to us that George-a-Greene is valiant, as long as he does us no harm? Envy seldom does any hurt except to itself, and therefore, Marian, smile upon thy Robin."

Maid Marian replied, "Never will Marian smile upon her Robin, nor lie with him under the greenwood shade, until thou go to Wakefield, and beat the Pinner on a green for the love of me."

"Lie with him" means "have sex with him."

A green is a public open area outside.

"Be content, Marian," Robin said. "I will ease thy grief. My merry men and I will stray there, and I vow here that, for the love of thee, I will beat George-a-Greene, or he shall beat me."

Will Scarlet said, "As I am Scarlet, second to Little John, one of the boldest yeomen of the crew, so will I go with Robin all along, and test this Pinner to see what he dares to do."

Much said:

"As I am Much, the miller's son, who left my mill to go with thee, and repent nothing that I have done, I say that this pleasant life contents me.

"In anything I may do, to do thee good,

"I'll live and die with Robin Hood."

Maid Marian said:

"And, Robin, Marian will go with thee,

"To see how bright fair Bettris is of blee."

"Blee" means hue. Maid Marian wanted to see how bright was the face of beautiful Bettris. This society valued light skin more than it valued dark skin.

Robin Hood said, "Marian, thou shall go with thy Robin."

He then said to Will Scarlet and Much the miller's son, "Bend your bows, and see that your strings are tight, the arrows have sharp, keen points, and everything is ready, and each of you carry a good bat on his neck, a bat able to lay a good man on the ground."

A bat is a staff.

"I will borrow Friar Tuck's," Will Scarlet said.

"I will borrow Little John's," Much the miller's son said.

Robin Hood said, "I will have one made out of a plank of ash wood, able to bear a bout or two."

Of course, he wanted a bat able to bear up during many more bouts than one or two.

He continued: "So then, come on, Marian, let us go, for before the sun shows the morning day, I will be at Wakefield to see this Pinner, George-a-Greene."

They exited.

— 4.3 —

At Bradford, a shoemaker was at work in his shop. Jenkin, carrying a staff on his neck, entered the scene.

Jenkin said to you, the readers of this book, "My masters, he who has neither food nor money, and has lost his credit with the alewife, for anything I know, may go supperless to bed."

Seeing the shoemaker, he said, "But, wait! Who is this man here? Here is a shoemaker; he knows where the best ale is."

Jenkin then asked, "Shoemaker, please tell me where the best ale is in the town?"

"Ahead of you," the shoemaker said, without looking up. "Just ahead of you. Follow thy nose, and you will come to the sign of the Eggshell."

The inn was named the Eggshell Inn. Its sign depicted an eggshell.

"Come, shoemaker, if thou will, and take thy part of a pot of ale," Jenkin said.

The shoemaker looked up at Jenkin and noticed that he was carrying a staff — which could be used as a weapon — on his neck. That is, he was carrying his staff in back of his head with his arms holding the staff near each shoulder.

46

Coming toward Jenkin, the shoemaker said, "Sirrah, down with your staff. Take down your staff."

He wanted Jenkin to hold his staff in one hand and let the end trail on the ground as he passed through the town of Bradford.

"Why, what is this now! Is the fellow mad?" Jenkin said to himself.

He then asked the shoemaker, "Please tell me, why should I take down my staff?"

"You will take it down, won't you, sir?" the shoemaker asked.

"Why should I?" Jenkin asked. "Tell me why."

The shoemaker answered, "My friend, this is the town of merry Bradford, and there is a custom here that no one shall pass with his staff on his neck unless he has a bout of fighting with me; and so shall you, sir."

"And so will I not, sir," Jenkin said.

He did not want to fight. But the best way not to fight would be to take down his staff, and he did not want to do that because it would be a sign of submission.

"That I will test," the shoemaker said. "Barking dogs bite not the sorest."

Talkers are not the best fighters.

Jenkin said to himself, "I wish to God I would be once and for all well rid of him."

He really did not want to fight.

"Now, what will you do?" the shoemaker asked. "Will you take down your staff?"

"Why, you are not in earnest, are you?" Jenkin asked.

"If I am not, take that," the shoemaker said, hitting him.

"You whoreson cowardly scab," Jenkin said. "It is just the part of a clapperdudgeon — a born beggar — to strike a man in the street. But do thou dare to walk to the town's end with me?"

"Aye, that I dare to do," the shoemaker said, "but wait until I put up my tools, and I will then go with thee to the town's end immediately."

As the shoemaker put his tools away, Jenkin said to himself, "I wish I knew how to be rid of this fellow."

The shoemaker said, "Come, sir, will you go to the town's end now, sir?"

"Aye, sir, come," Jenkin said.

Having arrived at the town's end, which was not far away, Jenkin said, "Now that we are at the town's end, what do you say now?"

"By the Virgin Mary," the shoemaker said, "come, let us even have a bout."

"Umm, wait a little bit," Jenkin said. "Hold back thy hands, please."

"Why, what's the matter?" the shoemaker said.

"Indeed, I am the Under-Pinner of a town, and there is an order, which if I do not keep it, I shall be turned out of my office and fired."

"What order is that, sir?" the shoemaker asked.

"Whenever I go to fight with anybody, I am to flourish — wave — my staff thrice about my head before I strike, and then show no favor to my opponent."

"Very well, sir," the shoemaker said. "Until you have done that, I will not strike thee."

Flourishing his staff around his head, Jenkin said, "Well, sir, here is once, twice."

He then held out his hand for shaking and said, "Here is my hand. I will never flourish my staff the third time."

"Why, then I see we shall not fight," the shoemaker said.

"Truly, no, we won't," Jenkin said. "Come, I will give thee two pots of the best ale, and we will be friends."

Bemused, the shoemaker said to himself, "Truly, I see it is as hard to get water out of a flint as to get him to have a bout of fighting with me; therefore, I will be friends with him for some good ale."

He said out loud, "My friend, I see thou are a faint-hearted fellow and thou have no stomach to fight; therefore, let us go to the alehouse and drink."

"Well, I am content," Jenkin said. "Go thy ways and say thy prayers. Thou have escaped my hands today."

Jenkin was joking that the shoemaker was lucky not to have had to fight him.

They went together to the alehouse.

— 4.4 —

George-a-Greene and Bettris talked together at Wakefield.

"Tell me, sweet love, how content is thy mind?" George asked. "Can thou endure living with me: George-a-Greene?"

"Oh, George," Bettris said. "How little pleasing are these words! Haven't I come from Bradford for the love of thee, and left my father for so sweet a friend?"

Bradford and Wakefield were approximately twenty miles apart.

This sweet kind of friend is a loved one, one she wanted to marry.

She continued, "Here will I live until my life does end."

"I am happy to have so sweet a love," George said.

George wanted to marry her.

Seeing some people approaching, he said, "But who are these people who are heading here?"

Bettris said, "Three men come striding through the corn, my love."

Robin Hood, Will Scarlet, and Much the miller's son walked over to them across a field of grain. So did Maid Marion, whom Bettris had not seen at first.

"Go back again, you foolish travelers, for you are wrong, and you may not go this way," George said.

By walking in the grainfield, they were trampling the plants.

"That would be a great shame," Robin Hood said. "Now, by my soul, proud sir, we are three strong yeomen, and thou are just one man."

He said to his followers, "Come, we will go forward in spite of him."

"Leap the ditch, or I will make you skip," George said.

"Leap the ditch" was an expression that meant, "Do what I tell you to do." It may have also literally meant leap over the ditch between the grainfield and the road.

He reasonably pointed out, "Can't the highway serve your need? Must you make a path over the corn?"

"Why, are thou mad?" Robin Hood said. "Do thou dare to fight three men? We are no babes, man. Look at our limbs."

Robin Hood and his men had big arms and muscles.

"Sirrah, the biggest limbs don't have the stoutest, bravest hearts," George said.

Not always, anyway. George had big arms, and he had a brave heart.

George continued:

"Even if you were as good as Robin Hood and his three merry men, I'll drive you back the same way that you came.

"If you are men, you will scorn to fight me all at once, three against one.

"But if you are cowards, then all three of you set upon me and test the Pinner to see what he dares to perform."

Will Scarlet said, "If thou were as high in deeds as thou are haughty in words, thou well might be a champion for the king. But empty vessels have the loudest sounds, and cowards prattle more than men of worth."

George said, "Sirrah, do thou dare to test me?"

"Aye, sirrah, that I dare to do," Will Scarlet answered.

Will Scarlet fought George, and George beat him.

Much the miller's son said to Will Scarlet, "What is this now! What! Are thou down?"

Much the miller's son fought George, and George beat him.

Robin Hood said, "Come, sirrah, now fight me. Don't spare me, for I won't spare thee."

"Have no doubt that I will be as liberal with my blows to thee," George replied.

They fought for a while, and then Robin Hood paused and said, "Pause, George, for here I do avow, thou are the bravest champion whom I ever laid hands upon."

"Stop, you sir!" George said. "By your leave, you lie. You have never yet laid hands on me."

"George, will thou forsake Wakefield and go with me?" Robin Hood said. "Two liveries I will give thee every year, and forty crowns shall be thy fee."

Liveries are suits of clothing that a servant or assistant wears. Robin Hood wanted George to become one of his followers, like Will Scarlet and Much the miller's son.

"Why, who are thou?" George asked.

"Why, I am Robin Hood. I have come here with my Marian and with these my yeomen in order to visit thee."

"Robin Hood!" George said. "Next to King Edward are thou dearest to me. Welcome, sweet Robin. Welcome, Maid Marian."

He then said to Will Scarlet and Much the miller's son, "And welcome, you friends of mine."

He asked them all, "Will you go to my poor house? You shall have your fill of wafer-cakes, a piece of beef hung up since Martlemas, mutton, and veal. If you don't like this, then take whatever you find in my pantry, or whatever you have brought with you, I say."

"God-a-mercies, good George," Robin Hood said. "Thank you. I'll be thy guest today."

"Robin, therein thou honor me," George said. "I'll lead the way to my house."

CHAPTER 5

— 5.1 —

At Bradford, several shoemakers were at work.

King Edward and King James, each of them disguised and carrying a staff on his neck, entered the scene.

"Come on, King James," King Edward said. "Now that we are thus disguised, I know there's no one who will take us to be kings. I think we are now in Bradford, where all the merry shoemakers dwell."

"Down with your staves, my friends," the first shoemaker said. "Down with them."

"Staves" is the plural of "staff."

"Down with our staves!" the disguised King Edward said. "Please tell me why."

"My friend, I see thou are a stranger here," the first shoemaker said, "else thou would not have questioned the thing. This is the town of merry Bradford, and here a custom has been kept for a long, old time that no one may bear his staff on his neck, but instead they must trail it all along throughout the town, unless they mean to have a bout of fighting with me."

"But listen, sir," the disguised King Edward said. "Has the king granted you his permission to follow this custom?"

"King or kaiser, no one shall pass this way, except King Edward, with his staff on his neck — no, not even the bravest follower who haunts his court," the first shoemaker said. "Therefore, down with your staves and trail them on the ground."

A kaiser is an emperor.

"What would be best for us to do?" the disguised King Edward asked the disguised King James.

"Indeed, my lord, they are stout fellows, and, because we will see some sport, we will trail our staves," the disguised King James said.

The sport they would see would be a fight between them and the first shoemaker. The disguised King James wished to avoid that sport.

The disguised King Edward said to the first shoemaker, "Do you hear, my friend? Because we are men of peace and because we are travelers, we are content to trail our staves."

The disguised kings were agreeing to hold their staves in one hand and let the end trail on the ground as they traveled through Bradford.

They lowered the staves.

"The way lies before you," the first shoemaker said. "Go along."

Robin Hood and George-a-Greene, both of whom were disguised, entered the scene.

The disguised Robin Hood said, "Look, George, two men are passing through the town, two vigorous, healthy men, and yet they trail their staves."

The disguised George said, "Robin, they are some peasants tricked out in yeoman's clothing."

Both George and Robin Hood looked down on men who would trail their staves as a sign of submission. Such men could not be of a higher social class than peasants. Yeomen would fight.

"Hey, you two travelers!" the disguised George called.

"Do you call us, sir?" the disguised King Edward asked.

"Aye, you," the disguised George said. "Aren't you big and strong enough to bear your bats on your necks, but instead you must trail them along the streets?"

"Yes, sir, we are big and strong enough," the disguised King Edward said. "But there is a custom kept here that no one may pass with his staff on his neck, but he must instead trail it at the weapon's point. Sir, we are men of peace, and we love to sleep in our whole skins, and therefore quietness is best."

To sleep in whole skins meant to sleep in skins not broken because of a fight.

"Base-minded peasants, worthless to be men!" the disguised and disgusted George said. "What, have you bones and limbs to strike a blow, and yet your hearts are so faint you cannot fight? If not for shame, I would drub your shoulders well, and teach you manhood in preparation for another time."

George would be ashamed if he were to fight such cowardly peasants. They were beneath him.

"Well preached, Sir Jack!" the first shoemaker said to the disguised George. "Down with your staff!"

"Do you hear, my friends?" the disguised King Edward said. "If you are wise, keep down your staves, for all the town will rise up against you."

The disguised George said to the disguised King Edward, "Thou speak like an honest, quiet fellow."

He then said to both disguised kings, "But listen to me, you two. In spite of all the swains — peasants — of the town of Bradford, bear your staves on your necks, or, to begin with, I'll baste — beat — you both so well, you were never better basted in your lives."

"We will hold up our staves," the disguised King Edward said.

George-a-Greene fought with the shoemakers and beat them all down.

"Have you any more fighters?" the disguised George said. "Call all your town forth, cut and longtail."

"Cut and longtail" usually referred to dogs: dogs with docked tails, and dogs with long tails. But George was using the expression to say that he would fight any men, no matter who they were, in the town.

"Cut and longtail" could also mean "vulva and penis." In that case, George was saying that he would fight everyone, women and men, in the town.

The shoemakers recognized George-a-Greene because his disguise had fallen off during the fight.

The first shoemaker said, "What! George-a-Greene, is it you?

He joked, "A plague confound you! I think you longed to swinge — beat — me well."

He then said, "Come, George, we will crush a pot before we part."

George said, "A pot, you slave! We will have a hundred pots."

He said to one of the shoemakers, "Here, Will Perkins, take my purse. Fetch a stand — an open barrel — of ale, and set it in the marketplace, so that all who are thirsty may drink this day. For this barrel of ale is a gift for all to welcome Robin Hood to the town of Bradford."

Robin Hood took off his disguise. The open barrel of ale was brought out, and they all began to drink.

George-a-Green said, "Here, Robin, sit thou here. For thou are the best man at the table this day."

He then said to the two disguised kings, "You who are strangers, place yourselves where you will."

Finally, he said, "Robin, here's a carouse — a large quaff — to good King Edward's self. I wish we had had a little beating of those who do not love him."

The Earl of Warwick and other noblemen entered the scene. They brought out King Edward's rich garments so he could wear them.

Recognizing their king, George-a-Greene, Robin Hood, and the others knelt down to him.

"Come, masters, we are all fellows," King Edward said.

On this day, they were friends.

George-a-Greene, Robin Hood, and the others remained kneeling.

King Edward said to Robin Hood, "Nay, Robin, you are the best man at the table today."

He then said to George-a-Greene, "Rise up, George."

George answered, "Nay, my good liege, ill-nurtured we were, previously."

He and Robin Hood had thought that the then-disguised King Edward was a cowardly peasant for trailing his staff behind him.

George continued, "Although we Yorkshire men are blunt of speech, and we are little skilled in court or such refined fashions, yet nature teaches us our duty to our king. Therefore, I humbly beseech you to pardon George-a-Greene."

Robin Hood said, "And, my good lord, I beseech a pardon for poor Robin. And I beseech for us all a pardon, good King Edward."

The first shoemaker said, "Please, give a pardon for the shoemakers."

"I frankly and freely grant a pardon to you all," King Edward said.

Those kneeling all rose.

King Edward then said, "And, George-a-Greene, give me thy hand. There's none in England who shall do thee wrong. Even from my court I came to see thyself, and now I see that your reputation is nothing but truth."

"I humbly thank your royal majesty," George said. "That which I did against the Earl of Kendal was only a subject's duty to his sovereign, and therefore it little merits such good words."

King Edward replied, "But before I go, I'll grace thee with good deeds. Say what King Edward may perform, and thou shall have it, it being in England's bounds."

"Say what King Edward may perform" meant "name your own reward."

"Being in England's bounds" meant "within reason."

"I have a lovely sweetheart," George said. "She is as bright of hue as is the silver moon, and old Grime, her father, will not let her marry me because I am a Pinner, although I love her, and she loves me, dearly."

"Where is she?" King Edward asked.

"At home at my poor house," George answered, "and she vows never to marry unless her father gives his consent, which is my great grief, my lord."

"If this is all, I will dispatch it straightaway," King Edward said. "I'll send for Grime and force him to give his permission for his daughter to marry you: He will not deny King Edward such a request."

Jenkin entered the scene and said, "Ho, who saw a master of mine? Who has seen my master?"

He had stopped being a magician and was again George's man-servant.

Seeing George and the others, Jenkin said, "Oh, he has gotten into company, and a body should rake hell for such company."

Jenkin was criticizing the people whom George was with.

"Be quiet, you slave!" George said. "See where King Edward is."

King Edward asked, "George, who is he?"

George replied, "I beseech your grace to pardon him. He is my serving-man."

The first shoemaker said to Jenkin, "Sirrah, the king has been drinking with us, and he did pledge us, too."

The king had drunk a toast to them.

"Has he pledged you?" Jenkin said. "Kneel. I dub you gentlemen."

"Beg it from the king, Jenkin," the first shoemaker said.

"I will," Jenkin replied.

He then said to King Edward, "I beseech your worship to grant me one thing."

"What is that?" King Edward asked.

"Listen in your ear," Jenkin said.

He whispered in King Edward's ear.

King Edward said, "Go, and do it."

Jenkin said to the shoemakers, "Come, get down on your knees. I have got it."

"Let us hear what it is first," the first shoemaker said.

"By the Virgin Mary, because you have drunk with the king, and the king has so graciously pledged you, you shall no more be called shoemakers; but instead you and yours, to the world's end, shall be called the trade of the Gentle Craft."

"I beseech your majesty *reform* this which he has spoken," the first shoemaker said.

"I beseech your worship *consume* this which he has spoken," Jenkin said.

Recognizing that both men had used the wrong verb — "reform" and "consume" — King Edward said, "You mean you want me to *confirm* it."

He added, "Well, Jenkin has done it for you, and it is sufficient."

King Edward had confirmed it: The shoemakers would henceforth be known as practitioners of the Gentle Craft.

The word "gentle" means "suited to people of good breeding, aka gentlemen." It also means "refined." Shoemaking was now a trade or craft suitable for gentlemen.

The king then said, "Come, George, we will go to Grime, and you will have thy love."

Seeing people coming, Jenkin said, "I am sure your worship will pause for a while; for yonder are coming old Musgrove and mad Cuddy, his son."

Seeing some other people coming, Jenkin then said to George, "Master, my fellow Wily comes dressed like a woman, and Master Grime intends to marry Wily. Here they come."

Old Musgrove and Cuddy, his son, entered the scene. Following them were Grime and Wily, who was disguised as a woman. Following Grime and Wily were Maid Marian and Bettris.

King Edward asked, "Which is thy old father, Cuddy?"

Pointing to his father, Cuddy said, "This man is, if it pleases your majesty."

Old Musgrove knelt before the king.

King Edward said, "Ah, old Musgrove, stand up. It is not fitting for such grey hairs to kneel."

Old William Musgrove rose and said:

"Long live my sovereign! Long and happy be his days!

"Deign to receive, my gracious lord, a simple gift from Billy Musgrove's — my — hand."

He showed King Edward a sword and said, "King James at Middleham Castle gave me this sword; this hand won the honor, and this sword I give to thee."

He gave the sword to King Edward.

"God-a-mercy, Musgrove," King Edward said. "Thank you for this friendly gift. And, because thou defeated a king with this same weapon, this blade shall here knight valiant Musgrove."

He tapped old Musgrove's shoulder with the sword.

"Alas, what has your highness done?" Old Musgrove said. "I am poor."

Being a knight was expensive. They were expected to have a horse, weapons, and a certain amount of income.

King Edward said, "To mend thy living, take thou Middleham Castle — take the stronghold from me — and if thou still lack sufficient income, make a formal statement of grievance to me, and thou shall have more to maintain thine estate."

He then asked, "George, which woman is thy love?"

Pointing to Bettris, George said, "This woman is, if it pleases your majesty."

King Edward asked Grime, "Are thou her aged father?"

"I am, if it pleases your majesty," Grime replied.

"And thou will not give thy daughter to George?" King Edward asked.

"I will give my daughter to George, if he will let me marry this lovely lass," Grime said, pointing to George's serving-boy, Wily, who was disguised as a woman.

In this society, masters had much control over their servants.

"What do thou say, George?" King Edward asked.

"With all my heart, my lord, I give my consent," George said.

"Then I give my daughter to George," Grime said.

"Then the marriage shall soon be at an end," Wiley said. "Witness, my lord, whether I am a woman."

He threw off his disguise and said, "For I am Wily, serving-boy to George-a-Greene, for whom to benefit my master I wrought this cunning trick."

King Edward said:

"What! Is it a boy?

"What do thou say to this, Grime?"

"By the Virgin Mary," Grime said, "my lord, I think this boy has more knavery than all the rest of the world. Yet I am content that George shall have both my daughter and my lands."

George would receive some land now as a dowry and he would inherit the rest of the lands when Grime died.

King Edward said, "Now, George, it remains for me to gratify thy worth and reward you as you deserve for what you have done for me by stopping Kendal's rebellion. And therefore here I bequeath to thee, on your full possession, half of all the wealth that Kendal has, and I give all the property that the monarchy has in Bradford freely and without restriction to thee forever."

He then said, "Kneel down, George."

"What will your majesty do?" George asked.

"I will dub thee a knight, George," King Edward said.

"I beseech your grace to grant me one thing," George said.

"What is that?" King Edward asked.

"To let me live and die a yeoman always," George said. "A yeoman my father was, and a yeoman his son must live. For it is more credit to men of base degree to do great deeds, than to men of dignity."

Men of dignity may be expected to do great deeds. Lowly born men may not be expected to do great deeds, and so they get greater credit when they do them.

"Well, let it be so, George," King Edward said, agreeing to the request.

King James of Scotland, who was still a prisoner, said, "I beseech your grace to settle my situation and set down my ransom."

Captured kings could expect to be ransomed at a great price.

King Edward said, "George-a-Greene, decide what will be the King of Scots' ransom."

"I beseech your grace to pardon me from doing that," George said. "It surpasses my skill."

"Do it," King Edward said. "The honor's thine."

"Then let King James pay reparations to those towns that he has burned upon the borders between Scotland and England, and let him give a small pension to the fatherless whose fathers he caused to be murdered in those wars," George said to King Edward.

He then said to King James, "Swear that you will do these things, and so return to Scotland."

"King James, are you content with this?" King Edward asked.

"I am content," King James said, "if it pleases your majesty, and I will leave good castles as security."

George had not asked for anything for King Edward from King James. Realizing that and knowing that King Edward would want more for the ransom, King James had offered to do as George wanted *and* to give King Edward some castles.

King Edward said, "I crave no more."

Her then said, "Now, George-a-Greene, I'll go to thy house; and when I have supped, I'll go to Aske in North Yorkshire and see if Jane-a-Barley is as beautiful as good King James reports her to be."

Finally, he said to the shoemakers, "And as for the ancient custom of *Vail Staff*, or *Lower Your Staff*, keep that custom always. Claim that privilege from me. If anyone asks for a reason why, or how, say that English Edward lowered his staff to you."

NOTES

— 2.3 —

Kendal. *Sirrah, those three horses belong to us,*
154 And we put them in,
And they must tarry there and eat their fill.
Source of Above: 2.3.153-155
Anonymous, *George-a-Greene, the Pinner of Wakefield.* Edit. Peter Lukacs.
http://elizabethandrama.org/the-playwrights/anonymous-plays/george-a-greene-the-Pinner-of-wakefield/
This information about Grain Overload comes from Horse Side Vet Guide:

> *Consumption of large quantities of high starch grain can have drastic consequences to a horse's intestinal health, causing digestive upset, abdominal pain (colic), and diarrhea. The most notable consequence of this occurrence is the development of* **laminitis (founder)**, *which might only become evident days later.*

Source: "Grain Overload, Horse Got into Feed Room." Horse Side Vet Guide. Accessed 29 September 2021

https://horsesidevetguide.com/drv/Observation/23/grain-overload-horse-got-into-feed-room/

— 4.3 —

And here hath been a custom kept of old,
That none may bear his staff upon his neck,
16 But trail it all along throughout the town,
Unless they mean to have a bout with me.
Source of Above: 4.3.14-17

Anonymous, *George-a-Greene, the Pinner of Wakefield*. Edit. Peter Lukacs.

What does it mean to "bear his staff upon his neck"?

It could mean to carry the staff across the back of the neck with one's hands holding the staff beside one's shoulders. Or it could mean to carry the staff on one shoulder by the neck.

Quarterstaffs are six to nine feet long, and if one carries the quarterstaff that way, one is taking up a lot of space on both sides of one's body. No wonder the shoemakers want the quarterstaffs lowered as the traveler goes through town!

More likely, in my opinion, the bat or staff is a walking-staff, which is shorter and could be carried that way. In that case, the shoemakers are either bullies or are simply letting travelers know that some people in town will fight them if necessary. The challenge can be a way of keeping the peace. Or fighting may simply be a form of entertainment.

George-a-Greene kills Sir Gilbert Armstrong with a walking-staff.

The *Oxford English Dictionary* defines "bat" as "A stick, a club, a staff for support and defence."

APPENDIX A: ABOUT THE AUTHOR

It was a dark and stormy night. Suddenly a cry rang out, and on a hot summer night in 1954, Josephine, wife of Carl Bruce, gave birth to a boy — me. Unfortunately, this young married couple allowed Reuben Saturday, Josephine's brother, to name their first-born. Reuben, aka "The Joker," decided that Bruce was a nice name, so he decided to name me Bruce Bruce. I have gone by my middle name — David — ever since.

Being named Bruce David Bruce hasn't been all bad. Bank tellers remember me very quickly, so I don't often have to show an ID. It can be fun in charades, also. When I was a counselor as a teenager at Camp Echoing Hills in Warsaw, Ohio, a fellow counselor gave the signs for "sounds like" and "two words," then she pointed to a bruise on her leg twice. Bruise Bruise? Oh yeah, Bruce Bruce is the answer!

Uncle Reuben, by the way, gave me a haircut when I was in kindergarten. He cut my hair short and shaved a small bald spot on the back of my head. My mother wouldn't let me go to school until the bald spot grew out again.

Of all my brothers and sisters (six in all), I am the only transplant to Athens, Ohio. I was born in Newark, Ohio, and have lived all around Southeastern Ohio. However, I moved to Athens to go to Ohio University and have never left.

At Ohio U, I never could make up my mind whether to major in English or Philosophy, so I got a bachelor's degree with a double major in both areas, then I added a Master of Arts degree in English and a Master of Arts degree in Philosophy. Yes, I have my MAMA degree.

Currently, and for a long time to come (I eat fruits and veggies), I am spending my retirement writing books such as *Nadia Comaneci: Perfect 10*, *The Funniest People in Comedy*, *Homer's* Iliad: *A Retelling in Prose*, and *William Shakespeare's* Hamlet: *A Retelling in Prose*.

By the way, my sister Brenda Kennedy writes romances such as *A New Beginning* and *Shattered Dreams*.

APPENDIX B: SOME BOOKS BY DAVID BRUCE

Retellings of a Classic Work of Literature

Arden of Faversham: A Retelling

Ben Jonson's The Alchemist: A Retelling

Ben Jonson's The Arraignment, or Poetaster: A Retelling

Ben Jonson's Bartholomew Fair: A Retelling

Ben Jonson's The Case is Altered: A Retelling

Ben Jonson's Catiline's Conspiracy: A Retelling

Ben Jonson's The Devil is an Ass: A Retelling

Ben Jonson's Epicene: A Retelling

Ben Jonson's Every Man in His Humor: A Retelling

Ben Jonson's Every Man Out of His Humor: A Retelling

Ben Jonson's The Fountain of Self-Love, or Cynthia's Revels: A Retelling

Ben Jonson's The Magnetic Lady, or Humors Reconciled: A Retelling

Ben Jonson's The New Inn, or The Light Heart: A Retelling

Ben Jonson's Sejanus' Fall: A Retelling

Ben Jonson's The Staple of News: A Retelling

Ben Jonson's A Tale of a Tub: A Retelling

Ben Jonson's Volpone, or the Fox: A Retelling

Christopher Marlowe's Complete Plays: Retellings

Christopher Marlowe's Dido, Queen of Carthage: A Retelling

Christopher Marlowe's Doctor Faustus: Retellings of the 1604 A-Text and of the 1616 B-Text

Christopher Marlowe's Edward II: A Retelling

Christopher Marlowe's The Massacre at Paris: A Retelling

Christopher Marlowe's The Rich Jew of Malta: A Retelling

Christopher Marlowe's Tamburlaine, Parts 1 and 2: Retellings

Dante's Divine Comedy: A Retelling in Prose

Dante's Inferno: A Retelling in Prose

Dante's Purgatory: A Retelling in Prose

Dante's Paradise: A Retelling in Prose

The Famous Victories of Henry V: A Retelling

From the Iliad to the Odyssey: A Retelling in Prose of Quintus of Smyrna's Posthomerica

George Chapman, Ben Jonson, and John Marston's Eastward Ho! A Retelling

George Peele's The Arraignment of Paris: A Retelling
George Peele's The Battle of Alcazar: A Retelling
George Peele's David and Bathsheba, and the Tragedy of Absalom: A Retelling
George Peele's Edward I: A Retelling
George Peele's The Old Wives' Tale: A Retelling
George-a-Greene: A Retelling
The History of King Leir: A Retelling
Homer's Iliad: A Retelling in Prose
Homer's Odyssey: A Retelling in Prose
J.W. Gent.'s The Valiant Scot: A Retelling
Jason and the Argonauts: A Retelling in Prose of Apollonius of Rhodes' Argonautica
John Ford: Eight Plays Translated into Modern English
John Ford's The Broken Heart: A Retelling
John Ford's The Fancies, Chaste and Noble: A Retelling
John Ford's The Lady's Trial: A Retelling
John Ford's The Lover's Melancholy: A Retelling
John Ford's Love's Sacrifice: A Retelling
John Ford's Perkin Warbeck: A Retelling
John Ford's The Queen: A Retelling
John Ford's 'Tis Pity She's a Whore: A Retelling
John Lyly's Campaspe: A Retelling
John Lyly's Endymion, The Man in the Moon: A Retelling
John Lyly's Galatea: A Retelling
John Lyly's Love's Metamorphosis: A Retelling
John Lyly's Midas: A Retelling
John Lyly's Mother Bombie: A Retelling
John Lyly's Sappho and Phao: A Retelling
John Lyly's The Woman in the Moon: A Retelling
John Webster's The White Devil: A Retelling
King Edward III: A Retelling
Mankind: A Medieval Morality Play (A Retelling)
Margaret Cavendish's The Unnatural Tragedy: A Retelling
The Merry Devil of Edmonton: A Retelling
The Summoning of Everyman: A Medieval Morality Play (A Retelling)
Robert Greene's Friar Bacon and Friar Bungay: A Retelling
The Taming of a Shrew: A Retelling
Tarlton's Jests: A Retelling
Thomas Middleton's A Chaste Maid in Cheapside: A Retelling
Thomas Middleton's Women Beware Women: A Retelling

Thomas Middleton and Thomas Dekker's The Roaring Girl: A Retelling
Thomas Middleton and William Rowley's The Changeling: A Retelling
The Trojan War and Its Aftermath: Four Ancient Epic Poems
Virgil's Aeneid: A Retelling in Prose
William Shakespeare's 5 Late Romances: Retellings in Prose
William Shakespeare's 10 Histories: Retellings in Prose
William Shakespeare's 11 Tragedies: Retellings in Prose
William Shakespeare's 12 Comedies: Retellings in Prose
William Shakespeare's 38 Plays: Retellings in Prose
William Shakespeare's 1 Henry IV, aka Henry IV, Part 1: A Retelling in Prose
William Shakespeare's 2 Henry IV, aka Henry IV, Part 2: A Retelling in Prose
William Shakespeare's 1 Henry VI, aka Henry VI, Part 1: A Retelling in Prose
William Shakespeare's 2 Henry VI, aka Henry VI, Part 2: A Retelling in Prose
William Shakespeare's 3 Henry VI, aka Henry VI, Part 3: A Retelling in Prose
William Shakespeare's All's Well that Ends Well: A Retelling in Prose
William Shakespeare's Antony and Cleopatra: A Retelling in Prose
William Shakespeare's As You Like It: A Retelling in Prose
William Shakespeare's The Comedy of Errors: A Retelling in Prose
William Shakespeare's Coriolanus: A Retelling in Prose
William Shakespeare's Cymbeline: A Retelling in Prose
William Shakespeare's Hamlet: A Retelling in Prose
William Shakespeare's Henry V: A Retelling in Prose
William Shakespeare's Henry VIII: A Retelling in Prose
William Shakespeare's Julius Caesar: A Retelling in Prose
William Shakespeare's King John: A Retelling in Prose
William Shakespeare's King Lear: A Retelling in Prose
William Shakespeare's Love's Labor's Lost: A Retelling in Prose
William Shakespeare's Macbeth: A Retelling in Prose
William Shakespeare's Measure for Measure: A Retelling in Prose
William Shakespeare's The Merchant of Venice: A Retelling in Prose
William Shakespeare's The Merry Wives of Windsor: A Retelling in Prose
William Shakespeare's A Midsummer Night's Dream: A Retelling in Prose
William Shakespeare's Much Ado About Nothing: A Retelling in Prose
William Shakespeare's Othello: A Retelling in Prose
William Shakespeare's Pericles, Prince of Tyre: A Retelling in Prose
William Shakespeare's Richard II: A Retelling in Prose
William Shakespeare's Richard III: A Retelling in Prose
William Shakespeare's Romeo and Juliet: A Retelling in Prose
William Shakespeare's The Taming of the Shrew: A Retelling in Prose

William Shakespeare's The Tempest: A Retelling in Prose
William Shakespeare's Timon of Athens: A Retelling in Prose
William Shakespeare's Titus Andronicus: A Retelling in Prose
William Shakespeare's Troilus and Cressida: A Retelling in Prose
William Shakespeare's Twelfth Night: A Retelling in Prose
William Shakespeare's The Two Gentlemen of Verona: A Retelling in Prose
William Shakespeare's The Two Noble Kinsmen: A Retelling in Prose
William Shakespeare's The Winter's Tale: A Retelling in Prose